A Christmas Stocking Story

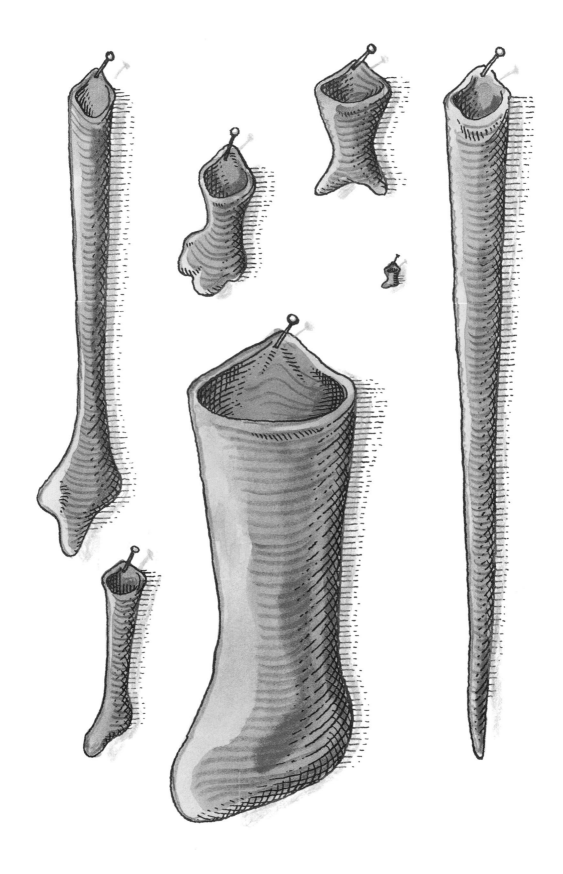

HILARY KNIGHT

A Christmas Stocking Story

KATHERINE TEGEN BOOKS

An Imprint of HarperCollinsPublishers

A Christmas Stocking Story
Copyright © 1963, 2003 by Hilary Knight
Printed in the U.S.A. All rights reserved.
www.harperchildrens.com

Library of Congress Cataloging-in-Publication Data
Knight, Hilary.
A Christmas stocking story / by Hilary Knight.
p.   cm.
Summary: When their stockings get mixed up while being washed one Christmas Eve,
a group of animal friends manage to sort out the gifts left by Santa Claus.
ISBN 0-06-000985-3 — ISBN 0-06-000986-1 (lib. bdg.)
[1. Christmas—Fiction.   2. Animals—Fiction.   3. Humorous stories.
4. Stories in rhyme.]   I. Title.
PZ8.3.K745 Ch   2003
[E]—dc21   2002010275   CIP   AC

1 2 3 4 5 6 7 8 9 10

First Edition

Happy and gay
as they could wish
lived Stork, Hippo,
Lion, and Fish.

Around a corner,
close and snug,
lived Elephant, Snake,
Fox, and Bug.

These eight dear friends,
one wintertime,
told this silly
Christmas rhyme.

One Christmas Eve
bug, bird, and beast
found their stockings
soiled and creased.

They quickly washed
their socks with care,
then looked at them
in deep despair.

Stork's stocking
was a soggy sack.

Hippo's stocking was
stretched and slack.

Lion's stocking
simply shrank.

Fish's sock
hung loose and lank.

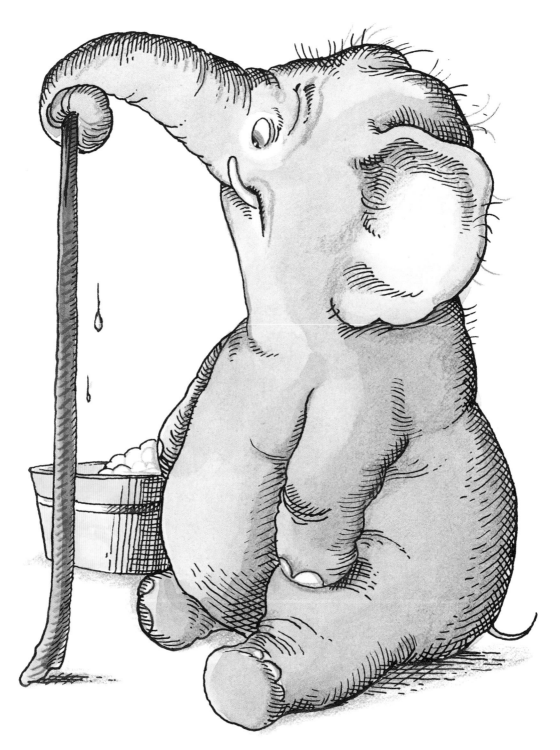

Cried Elephant,
"How oddly shaped!"

Snake said no word,
but gasped and gaped.

Fox's stocking
was *all wrong!*

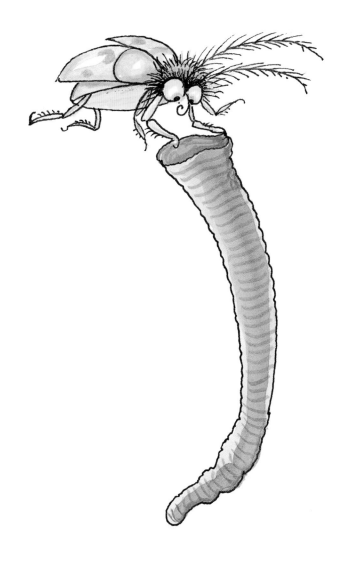

Bug's was much too long.

But they hung them up anyway!

When Santa Claus
appeared that night,
he filled their socks
by candlelight

with just enough,
but not too much,
relying on his
sense of touch.

When morning came,
bird, beast, and bug
each into his
stocking dug.

Stork, making
quite a face,
withdrew from his
four mitts of lace.

Hippo felt inclined
to grieve,
peering at
a knitted sleeve.

Lion, trying
not to scowl,
removed a
tiny Turkish towel.

Fish fell in a
solemn hush,
finding hers held
comb and brush.

Elephant, expecting
bigger things,
found his contained
six diamond rings.

Snake, hoping not to
show dismay,
discovered hers
was stuffed with hay.

Fox, never difficult
to please,
leaped when out
flew costumed fleas.

Bug was not
entirely chipper
as he unwrapped
a toenail clipper.

On Christmas Day
beast, bug, and bird
found each had what
the next preferred.

Stork said, "Let's do
our best to fix up
Santa's Christmas
stocking mix-up."

And they did!

Stork, who suffered
from sore throats,

wore his sleeve
with winter coats.

Hippo, hiding
giggling fits,

shyly showed
her lacy mitts.

Lion, looking
rather vain,

brushed and combed
his splendid mane.

Fish, springing nimbly
from her tub,

gave herself
a Turkish rub.

Elephant, who
loved to play,

wriggled in his
scratchy hay.

Snake, who yearned
for gaudy things,

slipped into
her diamond rings.

Fox displayed
his tidy feet—

all his toenails
clipped and neat.

Bug, crouched on
bended knees,

loudly cheered
performing fleas.

Now all was happy,
all was gay,

on this cheery
Christmas Day.

The End